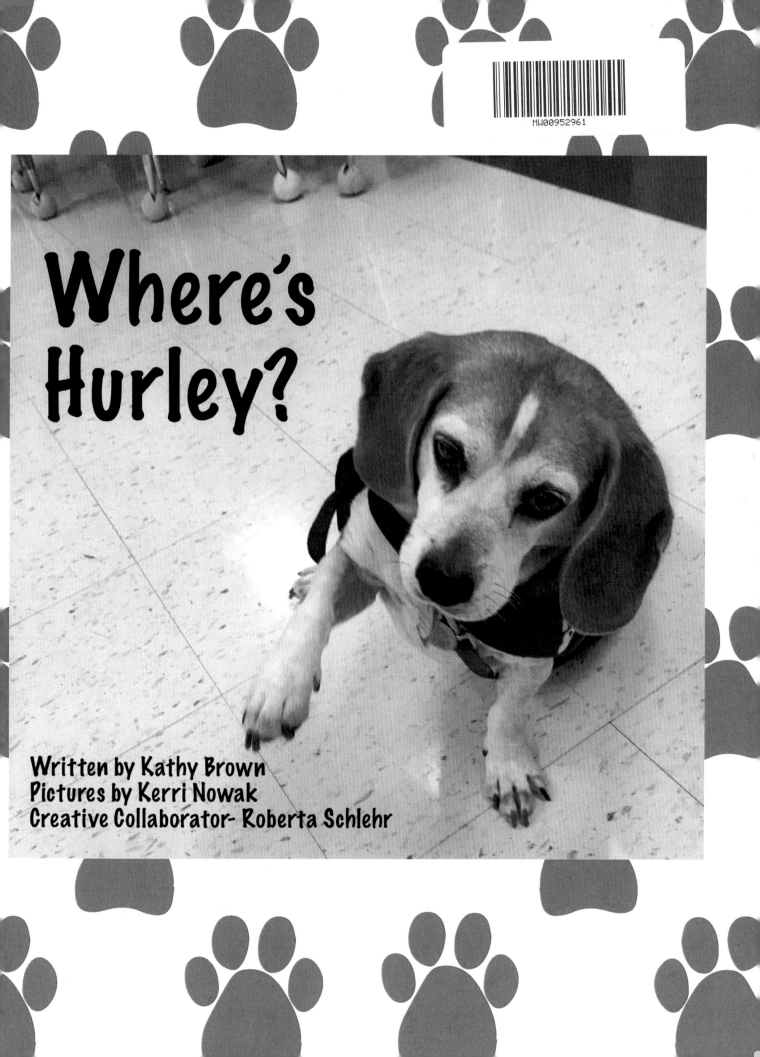

Where's Hurley?

Written by Kathy Brown
Pictures by Kerri Nowak
Creative Collaborator- Roberta Schlehr

Dedication

To all therapy dogs
and the love they give so freely.

"It is amazing how much love and laughter they bring into our lives and even how much closer we become with each other because of them."

– John Grogan
(Author, Marley & Me)

Hurley is an amazing therapy dog who comes to Huth Road Elementary School many times a week. Hurley is a beagle and everyone knows beagles are chow hounds.

They love their food!

He comes to school with his dog mom, Mrs. Brown and he goes with her wherever she teaches in the school.

Hurley makes school feel cool.

Hurley has made many friends in the school.

He sometimes sneaks quietly out of the classroom while Mrs. Brown is busy teaching to go find his friends.

Mrs. Brown then has to go find where he went in the school.

One day, Hurley went missing.

Mrs. Brown had to go and get him back.

As she went down the hall to find Hurley, students would stop her and ask, "Where's Hurley?"

22A
LIBRARY

NO FOOD
OR DRINK
PERMITTED

9

Mrs. Brown went to the Library because Hurley loves Mrs. Boivin.

She talks very sweetly to him and gives him very delicious treats.

But she and the children in the Library asked Mrs. Brown, "Where's Hurley?"

So Mrs. Brown had to keep looking for him.

Mrs. Brown was getting a little worried where Hurley might have gone.

So she went to the Main Office because Hurley had great friends there, too! Mrs. O'Connor gave him fancy, tasty dog treats.

But even she asked, "Where's Hurley?"

Now Mrs. Brown was really curious.

Hurley loves to eat but he hadn't stopped to visit any of these friends who give him treats.

There was only one more hallway where Hurley could have gone.

As Mrs. Brown passed a group of students, she asked, "Where's Hurley?"

The students said they saw him go by just a few minutes ago.

Mrs. Brown knew Hurley must be somewhere nearby.

She listened for his tags to clang when he moved but all she could hear was the soft crying of a child coming from the room ahead.

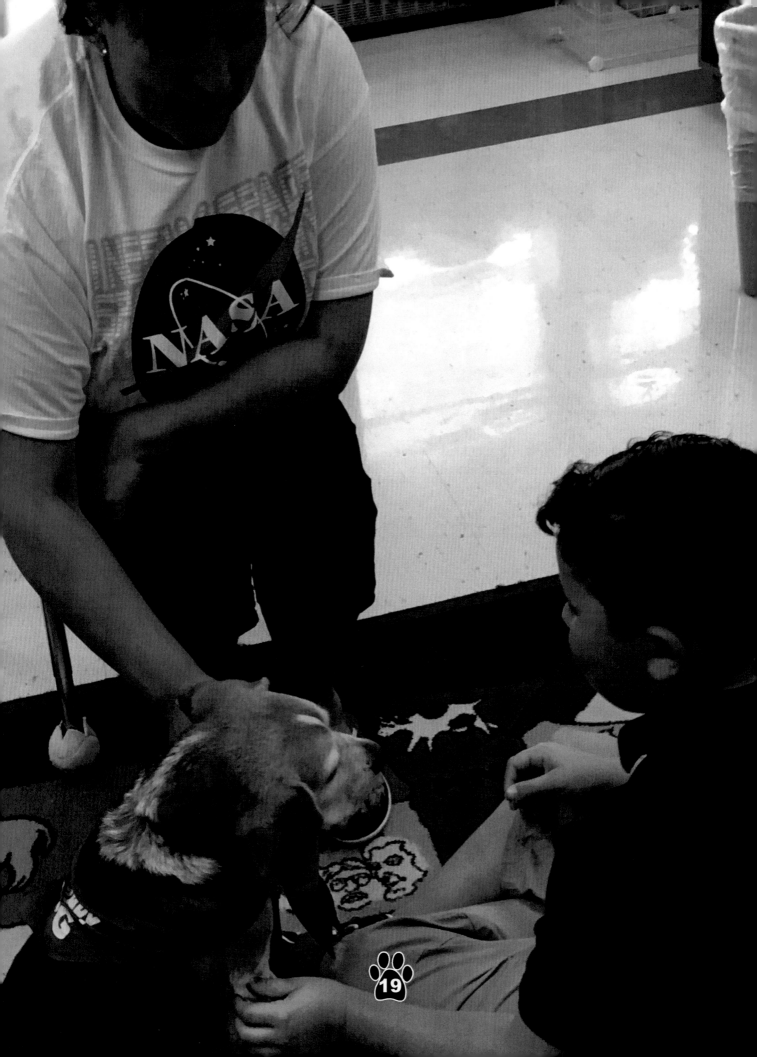

When Mrs. Brown looked in the room, she saw a small boy sitting on the floor petting Hurley.

He had stopped crying and seemed to have the beginning of a smile on his face.

The teacher with him was Mrs. Leahy who always has yummy dog treats in her desk.

The boy said he had gotten upset in his classroom because he had forgotten to bring in something for his turn at show and tell.

He had nothing to show or tell!

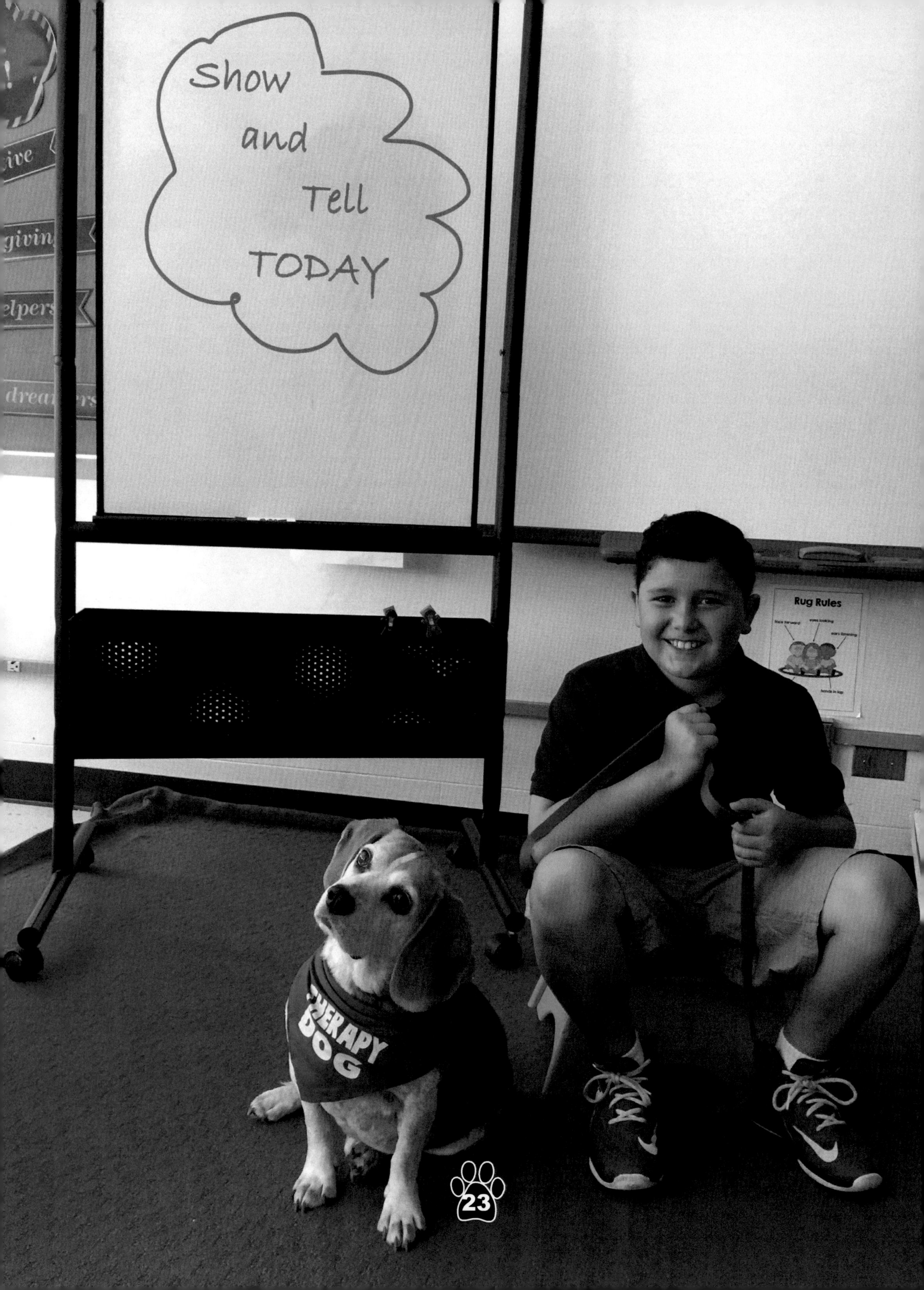
Show
and
Tell
TODAY
Rug Rules
THERAPY
DOG

Then the boy said with a laugh that Hurley had found him in the room and cheered him up!

The boy said he was ready to go back to the classroom, now.

Mrs. Brown asked him if he'd like to Show and Tell his class about Hurley!

Then the students would know how fun it is to have a therapy dog in school.

So Hurley and the boy went into his classroom and all the students got to hear the boy tell what therapy dogs do when in school.

They make everyone feel happy. Hurley knew he was needed and that made him happy to be in school, too!

Made in the USA
Middletown, DE
17 January 2019